For Janet

First published 1995 by Walker Books Ltd
87 Vauxhall Walk, London SE11 5HJ

This edition published 1997

© 1995 Colin McNaughton

This book has been typeset in Kosmik Bold.

Printed in Hong Kong

British Library Cataloguing in Publication Data
A catalogue record for this book is
available from the British Library.

ISBN 0-7445-4394-0

In outer space
It's black as night
And something's moving—
Speed of light—
Something looking
for a fight ...

HERE COME THE ALIENS!

Colin McNaughton

WALKER BOOKS
AND SUBSIDIARIES
LONDON · BOSTON · SYDNEY

A fleet of spaceships heads this way,
They're fifty zillion miles away
But getting closer every day -
The aliens are coming!

They're zooming in from outer space
To conquer us, the human race.
We'll soon be standing face to face –
The aliens are coming!

The admiral's a fearsome sight –
A simple creature, not too bright;
All he wants to do is FIGHT!
The aliens are coming!

The first mate looks like wobbly jelly,
He's sort of gaseous and smelly;
He has an eyeball in his belly!
The aliens are coming!

These beings come in different sizes –
This one's doing exercises.
Get ready Earth for some surprises –
The aliens are coming!

Some have one head, some have two.
(There's even one with none, it's true!)
What on earth are we to do?
The aliens are coming!

They come from planets near and far –
Some big, some small, some quite bizarre.

Twinkle twinkle, little star -
The aliens are coming!

I really hate to make a fuss
(Perhaps you thought they'd look like us),
But most of them appear thus:
The aliens are coming!

This one squeaks and that one squawks;
Some have eyeballs stuck on stalks.
This one squelches when it walks –
The aliens are coming!

See the aliens at lunch:
Slobber, dribble, gobble, munch.
Table manners? Not this bunch –
The aliens are coming!

Some are bald and some are hairy,
Some are roundy, some are squary;
Some look friendly but beware –
The aliens are coming!

They've boldly been where we've not been;
They're blue and purple, sickly green.
(At home this one's a beauty queen!)
The aliens are coming!

None speak English, French or Greek.
They sort of grunt and burp and squeak.

The chance of peace talks? I'd say BLEAK!
The aliens are coming!

Some have teeth and some are gummy,
Some are smart and some are dummy,
Some have ... HELP! I want my mummy!
The aliens are coming!

Some are tall and some are squat,
Some are cool and some are hot,
Some are nice but most are not!
The aliens are coming!

At last the Earth comes into view.
The admiral knows what to do.
He orders, "BATTLE STATIONS, CREW!"
The aliens are coming!

BUT!

Approaching planet Earth, they see:
(Though how it got there, don't ask me)
A piece of paper, floating free.
The aliens are slowing!

It's swiftly passed around the fleet.
A thousand hearts stop – miss a beat.
The order goes out: "FLEET RETREAT!!!"
The aliens are going!

For this is what the aliens saw:
A picture of your class – aged four!

It's scared them off - away they roar -
The aliens are going!